Be Careful, Little Antelope

Claude Clément
Adapted by Patricia Jensen
Illustrations by Pio

Reader's Digest Kids
Pleasantville, N.Y. – Montreal

The first snow of winter had just fallen, and all the young antelopes ran and played in the frosty air. They jumped from rock to rock on the snowy mountain.

All of them, that is, but one. Little Antelope wanted to play, but his legs felt wobbly and unsure.

"Come on!" his friends called. "Come and play with us!"

Little Antelope took a deep breath and started to run. But just as he took off for his very first jump, his legs slipped out from under him, and he took a tumble.

Little Antelope's father
ran to help his young son.
"Thank you, Papa,"
said Little Antelope as he
struggled to his feet. "I
guess I'm awfully clumsy."

"No, you're not," said Papa gently, comforting his son. "You just have to concentrate and be careful. Soon you'll be leaping as high as any antelope on the mountain. I'm sure of it."

Encouraged by his father, Little
Antelope called to his friends, "Let's race!"

Then he ran through a narrow rocky pass.
When he looked back, he saw that he was far
ahead of the others.

"No one will catch up with me!" he
thought happily.

But Little Antelope forgot to concentrate,
and his legs got all tangled up. He found
himself sliding down the mountain.

Little Antelope slipped and slid down, down, down—all the way into the valley. He finally came to a stop by an icy stream.

"How will I ever get back home?" he thought tearfully. "I'll never be able to climb back up."

Suddenly, Little Antelope remembered what his father had told him.

"Concentrate and be careful," Little Antelope repeated to himself. "That's the way to get back home safe and sound."

As he entered the woods, Little Antelope saw his friend the squirrel.

"Little Antelope," said the squirrel, "it's too cold for you to be walking in the woods. Why don't you sleep in my nest until spring?"

Little Antelope looked high up in the tree at the squirrel's nest. He knew that he wouldn't be able to climb the tree, and Squirrel's nest looked much too small for him anyway. "No, thank you," said Little Antelope. "I think I can make it back home."

"All right," said the squirrel. "But please be careful!"

"I will," said Little Antelope with a smile.

Little Antelope noticed that the sun was going down. He began to feel cold and scared.

Just then a groundhog poked his head out of a hole and cried, "Little Antelope! It's too cold for you to be walking in the woods. Why don't you sleep in my house until spring?"

But Little Antelope could hardly fit his nose into the groundhog's tunnel.

"No, thank you," Little Antelope said. "I will try to get back home."

"All right," said the groundhog. "But please be careful!"

As Little Antelope continued climbing the mountain, it began snowing again. He grew more and more tired, and soon his thin legs felt worn out. Just when he thought he couldn't take another step, Little Antelope spotted a cave behind some trees.

"I'll just rest inside there for a while," he thought.

Little Antelope trudged wearily into the cave, thinking about how good it would feel to nap for a minute.

Just then he heard a loud growl. Little Antelope looked up—right into the eyes of a huge bear!

Little Antelope dashed out of the cave and ran as fast as his legs would carry him.

"Concentrate!" he said to himself, jumping from rock to rock. "And be careful!"

Little Antelope bounded quickly and gracefully the rest of the way up the mountain. In no time at all, he found himself surrounded by family and friends.

"Where have you been?" asked his mother. "We've been searching for you!"

Little Antelope told them about his adventures and his narrow escape.

"Papa, all I had to do was concentrate and be careful!" Little Antelope said happily. "Now I can run and jump just like the others!"

"I always knew you could," his father said proudly as Little Antelope ran off to play with his friends.

The animal in this story is both like an antelope and like a goat. It lives in the mountains of Europe, where it is called a chamois (sham-WA).

Young chamois are very playful. They leap, frolic, and jump around in the snow.

Some chamois protect the rest of the herd by acting as lookouts to make sure that no wolves, hunters, or other enemies are near.